Mad Grandad AND THE

Robot Garden

*For my Mum, who planted my
roots in good soil and
nurtured me as I grew.*

Oisín McGann started making up stories when he was about six years old. For most of his childhood, he firmly believed that the world inside his head was far more interesting than the world outside it. As he got older and spent more time in the world outside his skull, he realised it was a lot more interesting out there than he had first thought. He went to art college for a few years and then spent time working at a bunch of different jobs, like making pizzas and guarding trains.

But he kept on writing and drawing ... and now he gets paid for making stuff up.

Oisín has made up more stuff about Lenny and his grandad in other *Mad Grandad Adventures*.

Mad Grandad AND THE Robot Garden

Oisín McGann

THE O'BRIEN PRESS
DUBLIN

This edition published 2016
First published 2003 by The O'Brien Press Ltd,
12 Terenure Road East, Rathgar, Dublin 6, D06 HD27
Ireland.
Tel: +353 1 4923333; Fax: +353 1 4922777
E-mail: books@obrien.ie
Website: www.obrien.ie
Reprinted 2006, 2007, 2008 (World Book Day edition),
2009, 2016.
The O'Brien Press is a member of Publishing Ireland.

ISBN: 978-1-84717-869-5

1 3 5 4 2
16 18 17

Editing, typesetting, layout, design: The O'Brien Press Ltd
Illustrations: Oisín McGann

Printed and bound by CPI Group (UK) Ltd, Croydon, CR0
4YY.
Thhe paper in this book is produced using pulp from
managed forests.

Published in

DUBLIN

UNESCO
City of Literature

CHAPTER 1

Grandad's Mad Garden

It was Saturday morning and I was helping Grandad clear up his **garden**.

Grandad was a bit **mad**. He spent
hours looking at things that weren't
really there, or arguing with the
radio, so he didn't have much time to
look after the garden.

I cut back some bushes and
found a headlight.

'Grandad!' I called. 'I've found
your **car**!'

'So you did, Lenny,' he said, coming over. 'I wondered where that got to.'

We cut all the bushes away and there sat his old car, which had gone **missing** a few years ago. It had not been missing at all; it was right where he left it.

'Well, I'm going to have to
take better care of this garden,' he
said. 'I'll lose the **house** in it
soon.'

'You need to get a gardener, or something,' I said.

'Yes, I do,' he nodded.

Then his eyes opened wide and he **slapped** his head.

'Holy smoke, Lenny!' he said.
'My brother, Rupert, sent me a
gardener from Japan! I forgot all
about it.'

CHAPTER 2

The Robo-Gardener 3000

Now, as I said, Grandad was a bit
mad, but he did have a brother
named **Rupert** (my great uncle) and
Rupert spent his time sailing all
around the world.

He often sent **weird** stuff back to
Grandad, but when Grandad said
he had sent a gardener, I thought
he was making things up again.

He took me into the house and down to the cellar.

The place was crammed with all sorts of stuff.

Under a load of boxes, there
was a **package** from Rupert. It had
stamps all over it and a note from
Great Uncle Rupert attached to it.
It said:

Hello from Japan!
Here's something to
clear up your garden,
Don't let it
have any nuts!
Rupert

We opened the box and there
was a **robot** folded inside.

'Wow!' I gasped. 'That's cool! I wonder why he says not to give it nuts?'

'Don't know,' Grandad said, 'but then Rupert's always been the **mad** one in the family.'

olded the robot. It had
Gardener 3000' written on its

'I think it needs **batteries**,'
I said.

Grandad found some batteries and we put them in the robot's back.

Then I turned it on. Its **eyes** lit up and it stood up. It spun around and rolled out the door.

We went outside and stopped
and stared. It was already hard at
work, cleaning up the garden.

It had all sorts of **gadgets** and soon it had cleared up all the leaves and was mowing the grass.

'Wow!' I said.

After it mowed the grass, it cut
all the bushes into different shapes,
like animals and birds. It clipped the
hedge to make it look like a castle
wall.

'Holy smoke!' said Grandad.

After it had finished with the bushes and the hedge, it pulled up all the weeds in the flowerbed and watered the flowers.

'This is the **best thing** I've ever seen!' I said.

CHAPTER 3

Digging in the Dark

We watched for another hour as it worked. Then, when it was finished, it cleaned itself up, rolled into the garden shed and turned itself off. Grandad wiped a tear from his eye.

'It's **beautiful**,' he said.

We had a picnic out in the garden instead of dinner, looking around at the **wonderful** shapes and colours.

When it got dark, we went in and watched some telly. Mum and Dad were away for the weekend, so I stayed in the **spare room** for the night.

A **noise** woke me in the middle
of the night. There was something
moving out in the garden.

I peeped out the window.
The robot was moving around,
doing **things** in the flowerbeds.

I put on my trainers and **sneaked**
downstairs. I quietly opened the back
door and looked out.

The Robo-Gardener had Grandad's toolbox open and it was planting something in the flowerbeds. I moved closer and saw it was planting **nuts** and **bolts** in the flowerbeds. Then it was squirting **oil** on them.

When I walked out to it, it looked around quickly and turned itself off.

I didn't know what to think, so I put the robot and the toolbox back in the shed.

Just to be safe, I **locked** the door.

CHAPTER 4

Nuts, Bolts and
Robot Daisies

The next morning, I woke up and saw Grandad standing out in the garden. I put on my clothes and ran downstairs. Outside, Grandad was **scratching** his head.

'What's up, Grandad?' I asked.

'Look, Lenny,' he said, 'all the

flowers are **gone**.'

He was right. All the flowers in the flowerbeds were gone. Instead, bits of **metal** were sticking up out of the ground.

As we watched, one of them opened and spread into a metal flower.

'Holy smoke!' Grandad squeaked.

'A **metal flower**!'

'They're **all** opening up,' I said.

One by one, all the bits of metal opened into flowers. There were small ones like daisies and pansies and big ones like roses. There were even ones that grew into **bushes**.

'That's what it was doing last night!' I gasped. 'It was planting its own garden. A **robot garden**!'

I told Grandad about what I had seen in the night.

'And Rupert said not to let it have nuts,' Grandad slapped his head. 'He meant **nuts** and **bolts**, not tree nuts! Well, now I have a **metal** garden. I suppose it could be worse.'

Suddenly, one of the metal daisies pulled itself out of the ground and ran across the grass to the shed.

It unlocked the door and the **Robo-Gardener** rolled out. More of the metal plants jumped out of the ground and started running around.

'I don't think gardens are
supposed to do this, Grandad,'
I said.

A metal rose bush ran up to us
and hit my legs.

'Ow!' I cried. 'It's got **thorns**!'

'Ouch!' shouted Grandad as
another rose bush bumped into
him.

More rose bushes crowded around
and pushed us towards the shed.

'Grandad, they're going to lock us
in the **shed**!' I said.

We fought back, but the bushes used their thorns and they hurt **a lot**. We ran into the shed and the door slammed shut behind us.

We heard the lock **snap shut**.

CHAPTER 5

Fighting the Flowers

'We're **trapped**,' Grandad said.

I looked through the window.

'They're planting more **nuts**
and **bolts**,' I said, biting my lip.
'There's going to be **thousands** of
them. They could take over the
world if this keeps going! We
have to get out of here, but how
do we get past the rose bushes?'

'I have an **idea**,' Grandad looked towards the back of the shed.

There lay all the gardening tools. Grandad started up the old lawnmower and I grabbed a pair of shears.

Right, Lenny. Let's do some **gardening**,' said Grandad.

He smashed the lawnmower
through the door and it ran over the
rose bushes outside, **chewing** them up
and **spitting** them out. I followed,
clipping the heads off the ones that
were left.

We charged out into the garden, but every time we cut one down, another popped up in its place.

'There's **too many** of them!'
Grandad cried.

Then I had another idea. 'We need
more **crunching** power, Grandad.
Does your car still work?' I asked.

Grandad gave me a look.

'**Great idea!**' he said.

We cut our way through the
bushes towards the car and
jumped in.

Grandad pulled out his big
bunch of keys and found the right one.

The car started with a **belch** and a **growl**.

Grandad drove **forwards** and flattened all the metal plants in front of us.

Then he drove **backwards** and
flattened all the plants behind us.

Then he drove around the garden
in **circles** until every metal plant was
lying flat and broken in pieces.

CHAPTER 6

Return of the Robot

There was only the robot left.
It stood against the garden wall,
staring at us with its little steel
and glass eyes.

Grandad revved the engine, but the robot suddenly turned, grabbed the handle of a **rake** and used it to vault over the wall.

'He's **getting away**!' Grandad yelled.

I jumped out of the car and
scrambled over the wall. Grandad
couldn't climb over it, so he ran
down the alley and out the gate
instead.

In the next garden, the robot was
making for the back wall. It tried to
leap up and grab the top, but it
missed and slid down into a
blackberry bush. It got all tangled up
and before it could cut its way out,
I jumped on it.

'Grandad! Quick!' I called out
as the robot fought to get free.

Grandad came through the
gate, but had to stop for a few
seconds to catch his breath. The
robot started to crawl out of the
bush.

Grandad was too out of breath to grab it, so he sat on its **head** instead.

I pulled the **batteries** out of its back and it went still.

'Let's send it back to Japan,'
said Grandad.

We folded it up, put it back in
its box and wrote on the top:

Then we took it to the post
office and posted it.

When we got back to Grandad's house, we looked at the garden. It was a **mess**.

'What are you going to do now?' I asked him.

'I'm going to get rid of all this metal stuff,' he said. 'Then I'm going to leave the rest. I've decided, having a **messy** garden isn't so bad after all.'

He went quiet for a second, then he said:

'But this time, I'm going to remember where I left the **car**. You never know when we might need it again.'